Laura's Star

Klaus Baumgart

"I wish I had a friend," sighed Laura as she gazed out of her bedroom window. "Someone special to share all my secrets with."

But there was no one listening, only the distant stars that winked and glittered like tiny jewels in the night sky.

Suddenly something caught Laura's eye. A streak of silver came whirling and twisting through the darkness. She gasped as it spun past her window, so close she could almost touch it.

Something wonderful and magical was happening! Laura quickly put on her robe and slippers and hurried downstairs.

Outside on the shadowy pavement lay a little star,
shooting sparks and colors like a giant sparkler.

"You're beautiful," Laura whispered. She saw that a point of the star had broken off when it hit the ground.

"Don't worry," Laura said as she gently carried
it back indoors. "I'll soon make you better, little star."
And up in her bedroom she carefully put it together
again.

Later Laura told the little star all her secrets. It seemed
to shimmer more brightly than before, as if it understood.

And as Laura drifted off to sleep, she knew she'd
found a special friend at last.

When Laura woke the next morning, the space on her
pillow was empty. The little star was gone!

Laura was desperate. She searched under the blankets
and scrabbled through her drawers. She looked high in the
closet and crawled low beneath the bed. But it was no good.
She couldn't find the little star anywhere.

Laura felt cold and empty, as if all the light had drained out of her. Surely the wonderful little star hadn't been only a dream?

When Laura came home from the playground, Mom and Dad tried their best to cheer her up. "How about your favorite dessert?" said Dad.

"Don't you like my funny hat?" asked Mom.

Laura couldn't tell them why she was so sad. They would probably say that the little star was just her imagination.

That night, as Laura climbed wearily up to bed, she saw a strange glow flickering from her room. Hardly daring to hope, she pushed the door open.

The sudden blaze of light was dazzling. The little star was back just where she'd left it, shining like a thousand diamonds.

At first Laura could only stand and stare. Then joyfully she ran toward it.

"I know what happened!" she cried. "Stars only come out at night. You must have been here the whole time, and I just couldn't see you. I should have known you wouldn't leave without saying goodbye."

Laura and the little star had a wonderful time.

They played games and did tricks, and Laura read
it her favorite book.

But Laura slowly noticed something. The little star
began to feel cold in her hand, as if it were fading away.

Laura stroked the little star gently with her fingertips as it grew colder still. She felt the longing in it, and suddenly she understood why the little star was dying.

Laura chose her four best balloons and carefully tied them to the little star.

"You'll always be my special friend," she whispered as she opened the window and let go of the strings.

Slowly the balloons drifted up into the darkness, and the little star twinkled at Laura as it grew smaller and smaller, until at last it joined the other stars in the midnight sky.

Laura didn't feel sad anymore, for her friend was back where it belonged. Each night when she went to bed, she could whisper her secrets into the darkness, knowing that the little star was somewhere out there listening.